SCRUFFY

*Illustrations by the Schoolchildren
of Bristol and Somerset*

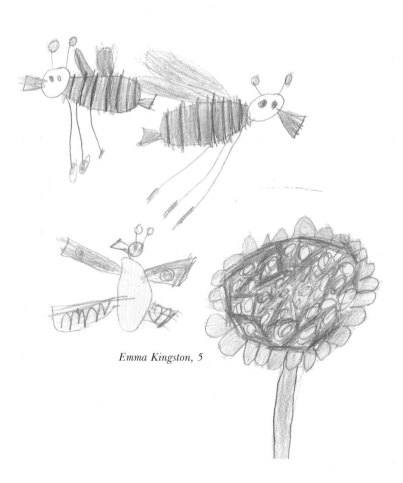

Emma Kingston, 5

HALSGROVE

First published in Great Britain in 2007

British Library Cataloguing-in-Publication Data
A CIP record for this title is available from the British Library

ISBN 978 1 84114 585 3

HALSGROVE
Halsgrove House
Lower Moor Way
Tiverton, Devon EX16 6SS
Tel: 01884 243242
Fax: 01884 243325
email: sales@halsgrove.com
website: www.halsgrove.com

Printed and bound by Stephens & George, Merthyr Tydfil

Ellie Richards, 8

A Visit to the Farm

It was Scruffy who spotted the car first. It had slowed, turning into the long gravel drive, which swept past the large pond, where a family of moorhens were living, and round the lawn, on which two huge cedar trees grew.

Scruffy should have been in his basket but he preferred to sit on Aunty's bed, where he could look out of the window.

Bethany Wright, 13

He was a bouncy sort of a dog, no particular make or model, but large and covered in a mass of black and white hair. Except that the white bits were usually black, especially when he'd been out hunting and returned home covered in mud.

Chloe Anderson, 8

Sometimes he even had bits of last night's dinner stuck to his whiskers. And you couldn't see his eyes, unless he lay down on his side, and even then only one eye – a big brown, friendly, understanding eye. 'Visitors!' he barked and leapt down on to the floor, his tail whizzing round and round in circles. He shook himself and hairs from his black and white coat flew off in all directions, making him sneeze.

'Hey Cinnamon, Ginger, wake up. It's most exciting,' he shouted, bounding down the stairs.

Scruffy raced through the kitchen and skidded on the slippery floor, crashing into the big kitchen table. The noise woke Cinnamon, who had been lying asleep on top of it, and she jumped up with a start.

When she saw who had woken her, she leaned down, her tail twitching angrily, and biffed him on the nose. Scruffy yelped loudly and hastily backed away, covering his nose with his paw.

'What did you do that for?' he said indignantly, rubbing his nose. Cinnamon might be a cat and she might be little, but she still had a fist like a sledgehammer.

Cinnamon glared – her eyes mere slits of yellow.

Then Scruffy remembered. 'Oh!' he said and slumped down on the floor. 'But I didn't mean to eat your dinner, Cinny, honest. It was an accident. It's just that I don't like to see food wasted. That's what it is. I like plates to be clean.'

'You know perfectly well I always leave a bit of my dinner to eat later,' the little cat hissed crossly.

'Yes, Cinny,' said Scruffy miserably. 'I forgot. But if you like, you can have some of my dinner tonight to make up.'

Cinnamon purred. 'Well then, you're forgiven. But you are such a sill-ee dog. Don't do it again. So why all the shouting?'

'Shouting?' said Scruffy. 'Oh! Yes, that's right.' He leapt to his feet. 'We've got visitors! Hurry up or we'll miss them.'

Scruffy bounced off through the woodshed, the pads on his paws like springy rubber balls. He skidded to a halt and fell over Ginger, who was

standing sleepily in the doorway, knocking him down in his hurry.

'What's up?' said Ginger, still half asleep.

'Visitors,' panted Scruffy, out of breath. 'Down the drive. Hurry!'

He tore out into the garden and round the side of the house, followed by the two cats.

Ava McBride, 7

The house was built of red brick and was very old. Once upon a time it had been a farm, with cows and chickens. Now all that was left was a large walled garden, where Scruffy played, and a big barn, where the cats hunted for mice. The house had three floors, with three big attic windows, and three doors: a front door, a side door, and a back door leading out into the garden. A very ancient wisteria vine grew up the side of one wall and, every spring, it was covered with green leaves like lace curtains, and trailing flowers like bunches of lilac coloured grapes.

Tilly Potter, 12

Scruffy bounded past Mr King, the gardener, who was digging potatoes.

'Morning, Mr King,' he shouted. 'We've got visitors. By the way, if you find any bones, they're mine.'

Mr King didn't appear to hear, too busy digging.

6

At the front of the house there was a white fence, which had been built to stop Scruffy going off hunting. He pushed his nose through the bars while the cats leapt up on top. They were just in time to see the car stop by the front door and a lady, followed by two young children, get out. The boy had sparkling brown eyes and dark brown hair. The little girl had brown curly hair and she was holding tightly to her mummy's hand. The front door opened and they disappeared inside.

'Children!' beamed Scruffy, happily. 'Come on.' He chased off up the garden again, followed by Ginger and Cinnamon.

'Morning, Mr King,' he barked as he raced past the gardener. 'We've got visitors and one's a little girl. Don't forget, if you find any bones they're mine.'

Mr King took no notice, too busy digging.

They chased back through the woodshed, and past the basket where Nutmeg and Clove, Cinnamon's new kittens, lay peacefully asleep. They ran to the big kitchen door and put their noses to the crack. They could hear talking and laughing and Scruffy's tail began to whirl round in circles, thumping against the wall as it went.

'Come on, open up, we want to see the children,' he barked.

There were footsteps and the big door swung open. There stood Kate, one of the family who lived at the Farm, the strange lady and the boy. Then Scruffy caught sight of the little girl, peeping out from behind her mummy's skirt, and grinned happily.

'Scruffy,' said Kate, 'this is my sister and her two children – Nick and Joy. They have come all the way from India to stay with us for the summer. Scruffy belongs to Aunty and he is the most marvellous watchdog,' she explained. 'Cinnamon and Ginger are brother and sister and they belong to me.'

The boy bent down to pat Scruffy.

'Hi Scruffy,' he said, in a voice that sounded like someone singing. 'Will you go for a walk with me?'

'Yes, please,' barked Scruffy, his tail wagging furiously. 'Can we go right now, I'll get my lead. Down the lane there's this fantastic field, full of rabbit holes …'

'No walks today, Scruffy,' said Kate. 'Aunty's busy cooking and Nick and Joy are tired after their long journey, and I want to talk to my sister. You'll have to make do with the garden today.

The big kitchen door swung to behind the family and the animals were left alone, gazing at one another in astonishment.

'That's very suspicious,' said Ginger, at last. 'I mean not taking you a walk. Aunty always takes you a walk, even when it's snowing. They must be very important – this family – for Aunty not to take you a walk.'

All the starch vanished from Scruffy's tail and it drooped downwards, like a wet flag. He sighed dejectedly.

Naomi Jackson, 7

Cinnamon climbed into her basket with her kittens. She turned and peered at Scruffy over the side.

'Well, it's no good moping, Scruffy,' she said sternly. 'Aunty will take you a walk tomorrow and you can play with the children then.' She sat down and started to give Nutmeg, who looked like a little black mouse, a good wash, while Clove, who resembled a ginger mouse, continued to sleep. 'And if it's raining, you can tell them a story.'

'What!' Scruffy yelped.

He sat bolt upright and gazed at Cinnamon, a horrified look on his face. 'Me! Tell stories! That's not work for a dog,' he grumbled. 'Can't I take them hunting instead?'

'You really can be so difficult,' hissed Cinnamon, her tail beginning to twitch. 'No! You can't take the children hunting, they're far too little.'

Scruffy sighed miserably and slumped back down on the ground, his nose on his paws. It wasn't fair; no one ever wanted him to go hunting and now no one even wanted to take him a walk.

'Anyway, you tell *very good* stories,' said Cinnamon. 'And there's no one else. Ginger is far too lazy and I am busy with my kittens.'

Scruffy sighed again.

'So that's settled,' said Cinnamon. 'If the children are bored, you can tell them a story.'

Faiza Hassan, 7

10

An Afternoon in the Garden

The two children gazed at Scruffy, who was lying asleep under the cedar tree. It was a lovely afternoon, very hot and lazy. All you could hear were bees searching the flowers for pollen, while larks sang overhead as they hunted for insects.

Naomi Dunbar, 14

'*You* ask him, Nick, you're older than me,' the little girl said at last.

'No, *you* do it, Joy, you ask him. He likes you best.'

Scruffy took no notice, pretending to be asleep.

'Scruffy,' said Joy. 'Will you tell us a story?'

Scruffy's ear twitched.

'Oh please do, Scruffy,' Nick called out. 'We're bored and Mummy says we have to stay in the garden till tea-time.'

Cinnamon strolled over to where Scruffy lay sleeping. A snore greeted her. She delicately lifted one eyelid and peeped in, to see if he really was asleep.

'Scruffy, you are to wake-up, it's bad for you to sleep so much,' she ordered.

Lucy Hooper, 11

Scruffy's other eye opened.

'Come on, you lazy dog, tell the children a story.'

'It's too hot,' he said and shut both eyes again.

'A STORY, A STORY,' chanted the children.

They made such a commotion that Ginger, who had been sunning himself on the fence, strolled over to see what was happening.

'Oh come on, old man,' Ginger said, adding his lazy voice to the children's. 'You tell such good stories and it'll help pass the time till tea. Tell us how you met Aunty. I like that story.'

Scruffy woke up and sneezed. He beckoned the children over into the shade of the cedar tree, with its canopy of branches that stretched out like fingers over the huge lawn. Ginger and Cinnamon, like all cats, stayed in the sun but near enough to hear the story.

Scruffy crouched down on his back legs with his nose resting on his front paws.

'I was born in Bristol town,' he began.

'Where's that?' said Joy.

'I don't know exactly,' said Scruffy. 'But I know you have to go there on a train.'

'What's a train?' said Joy.

'Be quiet, Joy, or we'll never hear the story,' said Nick sternly.

'I remember my first night away from my mother,' said Scruffy. 'The new people left me in the kitchen. It was cold and dark, and I was lonely on my own and cried ...'

Scruffy's Story – The New Puppy

The puppy's paws slipped on the shiny lino floor and he fell down, the fifth time since he had climbed out of his basket. Unfortunately falling down made him sneeze and sneezing made him fall over.

He sneezed – fell over – and sneezed again.

The puppy sighed and gazed at the door. It was an awful long way off. But his new family were on the other side and he was lonely. So he got up, on his four wobbly legs, and continued his shuffling run.

Anna Rigg, 12

14

Finally he made it. He put his nose against the door and pushed, but nothing happened. He pushed again. Still nothing! He tried barking, but all that came out was a tinny squeak. So he tried whining. That was a better noise – much louder – and he did it again. Then, for good measure, he scratched at the paint on the door. Now *that* was a really good noise.

Sasha March, 10

He scratched the door again.

There were footsteps. Someone was coming. Happy now, the puppy sat back on his hind legs and waited. The kitchen door flew open and the puppy flew head-over-heels back across the floor. He sneezed with astonishment and fell down. The man in the doorway laughed and, picking him up, put him back in his basket.

'Stay there,' he ordered and, tapping the puppy on his nose, went out of the room and closed the door behind him.

The puppy sat with his head on one side studying the door. His nose itched, where the man had tapped it, and his foot hurt, where the door had caught it.

Didn't the man understand he was lonely on his own? Well, he would just have to make him understand.

Georgina Munro, 12

The puppy put his nose and front paws over the side of the basket. Then, to his astonishment, the basket attacked him. It glued itself tightly to his tummy leaving his back legs waving about in the air. He wriggled about, trying to get his paws over the edge of the basket, and growled fiercely, biting at the wicker to make it let go. Finally the wicker basket gave in. The puppy slithered over the side and landed plop on the floor, spinning helplessly round and round in a circle.

He got up slowly and sniffed the floor. Fortunately, the floor didn't want to fight. So without any more fighting, the puppy – looking like an old man who was very drunk – continued his unsteady run across the kitchen.

He scratched and whined at the door, but it didn't budge. Then he heard footsteps.

Just in time he remembered how the door had burst open and attacked him. He turned and tried to run away. But, at that moment, the slippery lino floor jumped up and bit him. The puppy lost his balance and shot across the floor on his bottom.

This time the man didn't seem very happy. He wasn't smiling at all. He picked the puppy up by his scruff.

'Stay in your basket,' he ordered sternly. And, tapping the puppy on his nose, put him back in his

Daisy Tipping, 12

basket and covered him with the blanket. The door closed. There was silence.

After a while the puppy stuck his nose out of the blanket again and looked round at the empty kitchen. There was still that wide stretch of lino between him and the magic door. He buried his nose deep into the folds of the blanket to get warm. It was all very tiring; fighting, climbing and sliding about. He sighed. He did miss his family. Then he fell asleep.

The next morning the puppy woke up to a world full of noise.

'Blah – blah – blah,' shouted the people.

But he didn't understand.

'Blah – blah – blah,' shouted the machine in the corner of the room. The puppy didn't understand that either. He gazed at its flickering lights, his head on one side.

The girl picked him up and carried him outside. The ground was covered with white stuff and the puppy sniffed at it cautiously and prodded it with his nose. It tickled and he sneezed: 'Atchoo'. It was very cold but it seemed okay. He prodded it again. But when he tried to run, the white stuff stuck to his legs and wouldn't let him move. He rolled over and disappeared. 'Atchoo' he sneezed, when he came back up.

The girl laughed. 'You are funny, Patch,' she said. But all the puppy heard was: 'blah – blah – blah!'

After a few days he began to understand what some of the noises meant.

'*Dinner*' was his favourite noise. That meant a plate of food.

'*Good boy,*' was another. The humans made that noise, whenever they bent down to pat him.

'*Basket*' meant he had to get into bed.

'Come' meant he had to go to the person. And when he did that, he was rewarded with a biscuit.

But very soon, when the puppy heard the word '*come*', he looked first to see if there was a biscuit. If there wasn't, he didn't bother.

The puppy liked the lady, who gave him his food; and he liked the girl, when she sat him on her lap and stroked him. Sometimes he even liked the boy. Not always though. Especially when the boy picked him up and squeezed him till he couldn't breathe. Whenever he did that, the nice lady made a lot of noise.

'PUT PATCH DOWN, Jim, you'll hurt him

Calam Trunks, 11

squeezing him like that,' she yelled.

But he didn't like the man, because all he ever said to the puppy was: '*basket*'.

One day the girl tied a long rope-thing round his neck, which dragged him across the floor. He tried to fight it, but he was choking and there were bright sparks in his eyes. The girl picked him up and he could breathe again.

She carried him outside and put him down on some hard stone, which smelled horrid and was cold and slippery beneath his paws.

All around him were loud and scary noises like: plop – clunk – crash – boing – crunch – slam – oops – dong – clunk-click – brrrrrm – screech – ting-a-ling – nee-nu-nee-nu-nee-nu – meow – wuff-wuff – grrrr – hello! Mu-um, can *I* have a puppy, like that one?

Suddenly the puppy heard a most terrible racket

Jasmin Watkins, 13

and an enormous monster rushed past.
It was shouting loudly and left behind a
disgusting smell, which made the puppy
sneeze. He looked up, just as another monster –
just as noisy – charged towards him. The puppy
turned and tried to run away, but the rope-thing
pulled him back. He whimpered and cringed down
on the ground, too scared to move. Then he
remembered something his mother had told him.

'The monsters are people-carriers. They make a
horrid noise, but they won't hurt you if you keep away
from them.'

He watched timidly as the next monster rushed
past, shouting and swearing loudly, before rushing
away again.

'Come along, Patch. Walk nicely,' said the girl.

Bravely he got up and walked slowly after her.
After a while he began to notice there were lots of
interesting smells. But every time he stopped for a
sniff, the rope-thing dragged him along on his bottom.

'Hey, stop that! I like that smell,' the puppy tried
to shout. But the girl didn't understand.

At last it was over. The puppy climbed wearily
into his basket. His head ached from the noise, and
his bottom and paws ached from the hard ground.
He curled himself up in a ball and, next second, was
fast asleep.

Georgia Gabe, 11

Gradually, as the puppy grew, each day became a new and exciting adventure and he stopped being frightened. He didn't miss his family any more either, he was too busy having fun. Now he could jump straight out of his basket and play with the boy, growling and boxing, till they were both worn-out. Then they curled up on the floor and stared at the machine with the moving pictures.

And he understood so many noises, his family said.

'Why Patch understands everything we say. Goodboy.'

And now he had learned to make puddles in the garden, the door was left open and he could walk through and sit with his family.

Georgia Townend, 11

22

Lost

It was a lovely day, the sun shone and the puppy had been playing in the garden with the children. Now he was in the kitchen on his own, with the door closed. This was a bit odd because the door was never closed in the daytime now. He went over to it and scratched gently.

Upstairs he could hear the man shouting and then the children begin to cry. He quickly got into his basket, in case he'd done something wrong. But he couldn't remember chewing anyone's slippers and he was sure he hadn't made a puddle in the house. He thought and thought but couldn't think of anything. Still, he was always doing something wrong, so he stayed in his basket – just in case.

The man and lady came into the kitchen carrying some big boxes, which they took out into the front garden. After a minute or two they returned, without the boxes.

The man stood there looking at the puppy. He didn't appear to be angry, but Patch could still hear the children crying. He cowered down in his basket. *Something was wrong*, he knew it. The man picked him up and, taking off his collar, carried him outside to the people-carrier – just the man and the puppy.

Sophie Thompson-Smith, 11

23

They drove a long way. The houses disappeared and soon Patch could smell the strange scent of trees and grass. The people-carrier finally stopped. The man opened the door and put him down on the grass. Then, shutting the door again, he drove off, leaving the puppy alone on the side of the road.

Patch scratched his ear. *Was this a new game?* He waited patiently, but the man didn't return. Nothing moved. And now all the noises that belonged to humans were a long way off. Around him there were only the noises made by bees, busily searching the flowers for pollen, and birds chirping in the hedgerow. He lay down to think. This was a new puzzle. *Perhaps he had to find his way home? Yes, that was it.*

He got up and started walking, but he was soon tired and his feet became sore, so he sat down to rest. His insides felt very unhappy. It was like being a new puppy, all over again. He didn't know what the man wanted him to do and he couldn't remember which

Amy Tsui, 11

way the people-carrier had gone. He was well and truly lost.

By now Patch was hungry as well as tired. The man hadn't come back. Patch didn't know why and there was no one to ask. He began to cry. Then he remembered some advice his mother had given him: 'If you're in trouble, sleep on it.'

He looked round for a bush with nice soft leaves, not one of those horrid ones with prickly leaves that liked to scratch you, and scrabbled under it, as far as he could go. Then putting his nose under his paws, to keep it warm, he curled up and went to sleep.

Sophie Thompson-Smith, 11

It was dark when he woke and now he felt even hungrier, just as if his tummy was falling down. He sniffed about hoping to find something to eat, but there wasn't anything. He found a puddle of water and had a drink, until he couldn't feel his empty tummy any more.

The days passed, how many Patch didn't know. He found lots of houses, but he didn't find *his* house.

Most days he had nothing to eat at all. Occasionally he was lucky and found a rubbish bin he could knock over. He tried going up to houses and asking for food, but the people never understood. The dogs, that belonged there, could have told their owners that the puppy was hungry, but they were a snobbish lot, all smartly brushed and well-fed.

'Go away you tramp,' they jeered from the safety of their gate. 'My owner won't look at you, all dirty and scraggy.'

He tried to explain, but they only shouted more and pretended to be angry, barking loudly, until their owner came out and chased him away. They didn't want the thin animal, with matted hair, hanging around near their house.

Abigail Batt, 12

The nights were kind. It was warm and he found shelter in fields and under hedges, well away from the houses. He cried himself to sleep every night, wondering if he would ever find his family.

One morning, he was still lying half-asleep – even though the sun had been up for ages – when a boy walked past. Seeing the puppy curled up under the hedge, he picked up a stone and threw it – hard. The stone hit Patch on the head and he woke with a shock and jumped up.

'Hey, stop that,' he shouted.

The boy took no notice. Instead he looked round for something else to throw and picked up a jagged piece of concrete, which struck the puppy on his leg.

That was that, he couldn't fight boys with stones. Patch turned and ran off as fast as his three legs would carry him.

Hafsah Robleh, 8

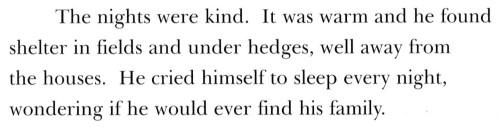

George

He couldn't go on. His leg was bleeding, his head hurt and he felt so sick and shaky he could hardly drag himself along. Instinct told him if he didn't get help soon, he would lie down and not get up again.

He limped up to a nearby gate and looked inside. There, in the yard, asleep in the sun, was the biggest dog Patch had ever seen. It looked like an overgrown mop-head, but much, much bigger, with a huge mass of brown and white hair. And there was so much hair, it was difficult to see where the dog began and ended.

Patch coughed weakly and said politely. 'Excuse me, sir?'

One eye opened and stared at him.

'Excuse me, sir, but I'm lost and hungry and I don't know what to do.' And he began to whimper, unable to stop himself.

A second eye opened.

'Well, what are you standing there for, boy? Give the gate a push and come on in, so I can take a good look at you,' roared the dog.

Patch could hardly believe his ears.

He hesitated just for a second then, making up his mind, pushed open the gate and hobbled up the path.

Charlotte Mounty, 12

'Well, I must say you look a pretty sight.'

Patch cowered down. He didn't know what he looked like, but he needed help badly and he really hoped the dog wouldn't chase him away, as all the others had done.

'You certainly need a good meal and whatever's happened to your leg?' Two bright eyes twinkled at the puppy, from underneath their covering of hair, and a huge laughing face beamed at him.

Hollie Biss, 8

'A boy threw a stone at me, sir.'

'*Ought to be a law against it*,' roared the dog, still looking very happy. 'Well, sit yourself down and tell me your troubles.'

So Patch told his story. When he got to the bit where the man had taken him into the countryside and left him, the happy face of the big dog changed, and he began to look serious – and then angry.

'Same thing happened to me, young man, when I was a pup,' he roared. 'The humans took me out and dropped me by the side of the road. Lucky for me, though, my owner happened to come along.'

The dog grinned, a wide, happy grin.

'Now look at me, grown old and fat from guarding the house night and day. Very strenuous job this, I can tell you.' He stopped to scratch an itch on his tummy and continued. 'Every summer

humans leave young whippersnappers, like you, on the road and go off. And every summer my mistress takes them in and feeds them,' he roared. 'Still, it's company for me. I look forward to the summer to see who's going to turn up next. *But there ought to be a law against it, there should.*'

'But why do they do it, sir? The family were very kind to me.'

'I expect you grew too big or they were going on their holidays. All sorts of reasons. Humans buy a puppy as a present for their children, at Christmas. And, in the summer, they leave them on the side of the road because they've become a nuisance. Same thing every year. Well, we'd better get you some food, hadn't we old chap.'

Patch nodded.

'Hey mistress,' roared the dog loudly. 'Come and see what we've got here.'

The door of the house opened and a lady came out.

'What's the matter, George?' she called. 'What are you barking for?'

'It's another of them.' George beamed, and wagged his tail as she bent down to pat him.

'Oh, you poor dear,' she said, turning to the puppy. 'Let me look at your leg.'

Patch cowered down, afraid she would hurt him. But she didn't. She had a good look at the jagged cut and then, without saying another word, went inside the house again.

'Where's she gone?' Patch whispered timidly.

'Oh, I expect she's gone to get some medicine for the cut,' said George.

Sure enough, after a few moments, the lady returned with a bowl of water.

'Don't move,' she told Patch and began to bathe the cut.

Patch felt so tired and ill he couldn't have moved however much it hurt. He sat there patiently, whimpering just a little when the lady touched the really bad bits.

The lady straightened up. 'That's better,' she said. She looked carefully at the puppy.

'Why George,' she exclaimed. 'He's going to look just like you. Are you sure he's not a relative wanting a free meal?'

George grinned happily, knowing the lady was making a joke. 'Come on,' he grunted. 'Can't you see the chap's hungry?'

The lady obviously understood. She disappeared into the house and reappeared, a few minutes later, carrying a bowl of biscuits and meaty gravy, which she put down in front of Patch.

It tasted scrumptious.

Patch gave the bowl a good set to and, when he had finished, carefully licked it all over, so it didn't have to be washed.

'Thanks, sir.'

'Call me, George. No ceremony here.' George beamed at the puppy through his forest of hair. 'Now, while you're at it, you'd better curl up and have a good sleep. You look all in.'

Patch lay down on the warm concrete and, with the first full tummy for weeks, fell fast asleep.

It was late evening when he woke. He yawned and stretched. Then he saw a bright eye watching him. He turned round and George grinned.

'Had a good sleep?'

'Mm! Thanks, George, I feel much better now.'

'That's the ticket. There's some more food over there. Hungry?'

Patch was. He headed straight for the dish, making short work of the biscuits and gravy inside it.

'What's your name, old chap?' asked George.

Georgia Townend, 11

Patch carefully licked all round his whiskers in case he had left anything behind. 'What's a name?' he said, looking puzzled.

'What noise did the humans make when they called you?' George explained.

Patch thought about it a bit, because his family had made lots of different noises: *Come on, Patch; Here boy; Good boy; Down boy.* In fact he wasn't sure whether his name was: *Come on, Good boy,* or *Patch.*

Georgia Townend, 11

'Patch,' he guessed.

George roared with laughter. 'What silly names you chaps have. You ought to have a sensible human name like mine.'

George looked very proud when he said this.

'Who gave you that name?' asked Patch.

'Why, my owner of course. When she decided to keep me, she said ...'

George stopped and got to his feet, beaming his smile, as the lady came into the yard.

'Well, George, and how's our friend this evening?'

'Oh, he's all right,' barked George.

Just to prove it, Patch put his sore leg gently on the ground and limped over to the lady to say *thank you.*

She patted him and scratched his ear. 'Okay, George, he'll do. Now, you look after him tonight and tomorrow we'll take him along to the home.'

She gave them both a last pat and turned to go back to the house.

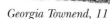

Annie Emery, 11

'Keep an eye on the house, George, there's a good dog,' she called over her shoulder. 'And, while you're at it, give our friend here an idea how he should behave tomorrow. Goodnight to you both.'

George got to his feet and, with Patch at his side, the two dogs had a good look round the garden, to make sure everything was in order. George took this duty very seriously and spent a long time sniffing at every bush, to check the garden was safe from intruders. After a last sniff, the two dogs returned to the front of the house.

'Well, as I was saying ...,' began George.

'Does she mean my home?' Patch interrupted.

'No, of course not, she means the Bristol Dogs Home.'

Patch asked timidly, 'What's that?'

'Why, it's a home for stray dogs, like you.'

'But what's a stray?'

'It's a dog that hasn't got a place to sleep,' George said 'The humans collect stray dogs and look after them, until they can find them a new owner and somewhere to live.'

Patch gazed at George in astonishment. 'How do you know all this?' he said.

'My owner works there,' said George. 'I often go to the home with her. I chat to the residents and keep an eye on newcomers, until they settle down. Sometimes, when my owner finds a stray, the van comes out to pick them up. Usually, though, she takes them to the home and, of course, I go with her. My job is to introduce the new chap to the other dogs.'

'Can't I stay here?' asked Patch unhappily. 'I wouldn't be any trouble.'

Charlotte Griffiths, 12

'Sorry, old chap,' said George sympathetically. 'I wish you could but she hasn't got enough dinners to keep two of us. You'll be all right. I'll go along with you. By and large the boys are a nice lot and my owner will soon find you a home of your own.'

Poor Patch. All he wanted was to stay in the lady's yard and get well again. He didn't want to go to the strange home. But if George said it would be okay, then it would be.

Annabel Drauschte, 13

'Couple of things you should know,' George rumbled on. 'The best way to find a new family is to behave well at the home. And another thing, never let on what you're thinking. You're lucky. When you're older, you'll be covered with hair, and humans won't be able to see your face. And keep cheerful, a cheerful dog never upset anyone.' And George's eyes twinkled and all of his face laughed.

Patch lay quietly. He still couldn't believe his luck. Only that morning he'd been lost and starving and now he had a most wonderful friend.

'Hmm,' he grunted to himself. 'And when I grow up, I'm going to be exactly like George.'

And with that Patch was fast sleep.

Bathtime

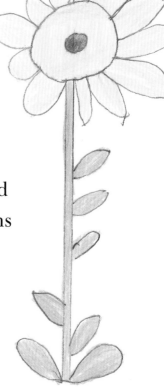

When Patch woke up the sun was shining brightly. He'd been having a lovely dream, living in a house full of delicious biscuits and gravy. He lifted his head and saw George, looking very happy, tucking into a huge breakfast. The lady was washing the people carrier.

'Good morning,' grunted George between mouthfuls. 'Breakfast's over here. Didn't wake you before. Thought you needed the rest. Fresh water in the bowl.'

Patch had a good drink and headed for his breakfast. He ate in total silence, until his bowl was nearly empty.

'George?' he asked with his mouth full. 'What's Bristol?'

'A big town,' came George's muffled reply.

'What's a town?'

'A place full of houses where humans live,' said George. He stopped eating and sat down, so he could explain better. 'My owner says lots and lots of humans live in Bristol. You'll see how big it is when we go to the home. That's why they have cars, to get from one side of the town to the other.'

'What's a car?' asked Patch.

'That's one,' said George, nodding towards the

people-carrier.

Patch gazed at him in admiration. 'But how do you know so much?' he said.

George yawned and scratched his ear with a huge paw.

'I've seen a lot and remember I'm not young, either. And I go everywhere with my owner. She talks to me all the time.'

'And you understand?'

'Every word!' roared George proudly. 'Of course, it wasn't easy at first, but if you listen hard you begin to understand. She talks to me about everything. She said I'm an Old English Sheep Dog.'

'What's that?' asked Patch, anxious to learn.

'It's a type of dog that is used to guard sheep. Lots of sheep dogs are covered with hair, like me.'

He turned and nodded his head in the direction of the fence. 'Do you see that thing next door?'

Patch got up and limped over to the fence.

A dog, much, much smaller than him, with fluffy white hair, rushed up shrieking. 'Go away, go away, you horrible monster, go away.' It rushed back across the garden, its legs bouncing in the air.

'That's Felicity. She's a poodle,' said George. 'Poodles are supposed to be hunting dogs. But you should see Felicity run when a cat appears – hunting dog, my foot.'

'George, do you know what I am?' asked Patch nervously.

'You?' George sounded surprised. 'I've never seen anything quite like you before. Of course, you're not full grown and terribly thin, but still ...'

George walked all round Patch, looking at him first from one side and then the other. He grinned. 'If you ask me, I'd say you were the result of a fight and they stuck together all the bits that were left.'

Sarah Buddle, 8

'You mean I'm not like you?'

'Like me! Whatever gave you that idea?' George went back to finish his breakfast.

'Well,' Patch sat down on the pathway, very upset, 'the lady said ...'

'Oh that. No, you'll be smaller than me and a different shape and colour. There must be a bit of sheepdog in you, but I don't know what the rest is. Still, when you're cleaned up, you'll have character and that's better than looks anytime.'

George yawned. 'I was telling you how I got my name. My owner lives alone. If someone comes to the door and she doesn't like them, she says: *Just a minute, I'll fetch George He'll decide.* Of course, they think there's another human in the house and go away. Not that anyone would get past me. Anyway one day ...'

While George rambled on, Patch was watching the lady. She had finished washing the car and was now pouring water into a large bowl, and adding some white stuff to it.

'What's she doing now?' asked Patch interrupting George's story.

'Fixing you a bath. You can't go to the home smelling like that,' said George, suddenly sounding very sleepy.

'What's a bath?'

There was no reply. Eating breakfast was very tiring work and George was fast asleep.

The lady walked across the yard and picked Patch up. She carried him to the bowl and put him down in the warm water, taking care not to hurt his bad leg. He struggled and some of the white stuff went into his eyes, and made them sting.

'Help! Help! I can't see. I'm being attacked,' he shouted. He wriggled about trying to get free.

'Now don't be a silly dog. Stop wriggling. You've got to be washed.'

The lady held him firmly in the water, putting more soap over his back. There were bubbles floating in the air, which made Patch's nose tickle. He sneezed.

'Atchoo! George?' he called. 'Help me? I'm being attacked. Atchoo!'

Belinda Amey, 14

George woke up and looked across at Patch, who had one ear up, one ear down, and only one eye open.

'Stop struggling, Patch, it's only water and it's nice if you don't struggle,' he roared.

Patch felt more water being poured over his back and then he was free. He climbed clumsily out of the bath and shook himself to get rid of the water. The drops flew everywhere, even landing on George's nose. He licked them off and went back to sleep.

When Patch's coat had dried a bit, the lady got a brush and started to brush him. It felt wonderful. By the time she had finished, Patch tingled all the way from his nose to his tail and he felt strong enough to jump at George, as a punishment for laughing at him. George woke up then and, putting out a paw, knocked Patch down. Then the two dogs went rolling round and round the yard, while the lady looked on and laughed.

April Wilson, 12

42

The Home for Stray Dogs

On the way to the home, George sat in the front of the car, while Patch sat in a special compartment at the back. He looked out, gazing with amazement at streets and streets full of houses.

'Is this all Bristol?' he asked.

'Yes,' replied George. 'Told you it was big, didn't I?'

Ellen Murphy, 11

George sounded his usual cheerful self, but Patch felt nervous and worried inside. They drove into the home and he heard dozens of cats and dogs – all talking and shouting.

A man met them and, putting Patch on a lead, took him into a big building, full of bright lights, where people were working. He opened the door of a big white room where a lady, in a white coat, was waiting for them. She picked Patch up and put him gently down on a large table.

Patch *was* astonished. Whenever he had tried to get up on his family's table, he had his nose tapped. He *even* had his nose tapped for putting a paw on the table. Now here he was, standing on one.

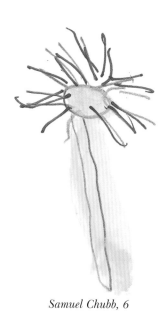

Samuel Chubb, 6

The lady looked at his leg, which still hurt very much. Then she looked in his ears and his mouth. Then she attacked him with something long and thin, and so sharp, it really hurt. Patch jumped and squealed, and instantly decided he didn't like the lady any more. She patted him and put him back on the floor.

'That's all I can do for him, poor fellow,' she said to George's owner. 'He's so emaciated, it'll be weeks before he's fit again.'

Patch was put back on his lead and taken out into a large paved courtyard, where rows and rows of wire-mesh cages had been built, to house the stray animals.

44

Lauren Edwards, 10

As they walked between the long rows of cages, dogs rushed over to the wire, barking madly, all of them wanting to say hello to George. The noise was deafening. George nodded and beamed cheerfully, occasionally stopping to have a word with a friend.

He stopped by the open gate of a small yard and peered through his fringe at the three dogs, who were to be Patch's new companions.

'Well, boys,' he called heartily. 'This is Patch. He's a friend of mine.'

The three dogs looked a pretty rough lot, with no breeding or education at all. They'd not been long at the home themselves and had been found roaming the streets of Bristol, where they had lived from the time they were born. Their coats were mangy and their tails thin and scrawny, and fixed permanently between their legs, as if they had spent their entire

Jessica Roberts, 12

lives running away from rocks and stones.

'Well,' sneered a whitish-coloured dog with a black patch on his eye. 'Just look what the cat's brought in.'

The other two tittered, lowering their heads aggressively.

'Enough of that sort of talk,' said George sharply. 'He's a stray like you. So remember your manners or I'll teach you some.'

Patch hesitated. He didn't like the look of the three dogs, with their sharp eyes staring at him – never blinking. Reluctantly he put a paw into the yard. He caught their sneering glance and backed away.

'George,' he whispered. 'I'm scared.'

He felt a strange sensation on his back, unlike anything he'd felt before, as if his skin was being pricked with thousands of needles, and the hairs on the back of his neck stood straight up.

He heard George shout, 'Look out!' But it was too late.

The dogs were at him, all teeth and claws, snarling and spitting. It was all too sudden and Patch was flung to the ground. There were teeth in his neck, biting and twisting, and he struggled to breathe.

Suddenly his attacker flew into the air and, losing his hold on Patch's neck, ran screaming into the corner followed by his two cringing followers.

It was George. With one tremendous blow of his paw he had knocked all three dogs across the yard.

George bent his head to look at the wound on Patch's neck and licked it. 'You okay, old chap?' he said.

Patch was too shocked and breathless to reply. He lay there trembling all over. George got him to his feet.

'You can't stay here, that's certain,' he said. And, with a last ferocious glare at the three dogs, cowering away from him in the corner, George helped Patch out of the yard and out of danger.

The man locked the gate behind them and they continued down the pathway. At the far end of the row was a large yard, with a number of dogs milling around. A Jack Russell ran to the wire fence, barking excitedly.

'He'd better go in here,' the man said to George's owner, who looked very upset. 'The Alsatian will take care of him.'

She nodded thankfully and turned to look back at George, who was walking with Patch and helping him along. As they approached the yard, George looked up and saw the Alsatian.

'Good morning, Prince,' he called through the fence. 'Look after my friend here. He got a rough welcome up the path.'

A stately looking dog trotted over and put his nose to the railings. He wasn't as large as George but his legs were longer and his hair, which lay thickly on his flanks, was short and brown-gold in colour. He had a very responsible air about him.

'So that's what the noise was,' said Prince. 'I did wonder if it was those tramps, from the slums, creating trouble again. They just never learn.'

He studied Patch, who stood with his head down, exhausted and shaking all over.

Victoria Berryman, 13

'Good morning, young man, you are most welcome,' he said. 'There's no fighting allowed and no swearing in front of the ladies. A friend you said, George?'

George nodded. 'Mm! Good chap too and only a youngster. Had a bad time, pretty hungry, you know. I'd be obliged if you'd keep an eye on him. I'll drop by, from time to time, to see how he's settling down.'

He helped Patch into the grassy yard and turned to go. The man locked the gate after him, locking Patch securely inside.

'Cheerio, Patch,' George called. 'Got to go now but you'll be right as rain with Prince. Keep out of trouble – that's the ticket.'

George swung on his heel following his owner and, in a second, had disappeared from sight.

'George,' cried Patch pushing his nose through the holes in the wire. 'George, don't leave me, I'm frightened.'

He called and called but George didn't return. Patch started to cry. His neck hurt where he'd been bitten, his leg hurt too, and he felt lost all over again.

'Now, young man, no crying please,' said Prince firmly. 'It will disturb the others. After all, we're all strays here.'

Patch whimpered a bit and then stopped and was quiet.

'Very good. Now there's no need to be frightened. Come along, I will introduce you to the other members of our yard.'

The other dogs in the yard were all very respectful towards the Alsatian, standing to attention and calling him *sir*. The eldest, Daisy, was a boxer. She had rheumatism in her back legs, and liked to sit in the sun to keep warm. Joe, her best friend, was a dachshund, and so little he could walk under Daisy's legs. There was a wire-haired terrier, with a rough greyish-white jacket, who had forgotten his name; and a smooth-haired terrier, with a tan jacket with

49

black patches, who was so nervous he trembled all the time. And, last of all, there was Fred, the very noisy Jack Russell, who jumped high into the air whenever he barked.

Prince showed Patch where he was to sleep and explained the rules of the yard. Then he sat down by Patch's side, so the puppy could rest on the ground. Prince spoke seriously, but not loudly, and in a little while Patch began to feel more comfortable.

'Have you been here a long time, sir?' he asked timidly.

'About three seasons, I should think,' said Prince calmly.

'Three seasons!' Patch was horrified. 'But George said I would soon find a new home.'

'Well, so you might, but I am an Alsatian. We're different.'

Zoe Slocombe, 11

'Excuse me, sir, but what's an Alsatian?'

'Do you understand that George is called an Old English Sheep Dog?'

Patch nodded.

'That is George's breed. Some dogs are a mixture of breeds but I am, what is called, a thoroughbred. That means I have only the one breed, which is Alsatian. Sadly people are often frightened of us, and it will be difficult to find me a new home.' Prince looked very proud – but sad – when he said this.

'Are you dangerous then?' asked Patch.

'Dangerous? No, not at all,' said Prince. 'However, many of us look like wolves, which are big wild dogs that attack humans. That is why people are afraid. And we *are* very strong and brave.'

Tom Clark, 9

'And will you stay here for always, sir?'

Prince shook his head. 'I don't think so. George told me that his owner had been talking to the police about me. He says they have agreed to take me for a police dog.'

Now Patch didn't know what a '*police*' was, but he didn't want to look foolish, so he nodded and pretended he understood.

Prince got to his feet. 'Now, young man,' he said kindly, 'the more sleep you get in the next few days, the quicker you will get better. I will call you when dinner comes.'

Over the next few weeks Prince kept his word to George and kept more than one eye on Patch. He made sure Patch had a fair ration of food, and the other dogs left him alone.

But even Prince couldn't do anything about the noise. Dogs barking and howling, cats yowling, doors slamming, people talking and laughing; it made Patch feel horribly sick and trembly. For the emaciated

puppy, the noise was far worse than even the rampaging monsters he had met on his first walk. George called to see him every few days, but Patch knew, without the help of Prince and George, he would not have survived life in the yard.

It took about a month but, little by little, Patch began to feel stronger and then, he began to settle down to his new life. He still found the noise upsetting, but the other dogs in the grassy yard were a kindly lot and he made some friends.

And sometimes he was put on a lead and taken for a real walk – outside the home. Here he could smell different and exciting scents and, despite the cars rushing past, it was quiet. And Patch loved going for walks so much he wished it could happen every day.

Emily Hayward, 9

The Police Dog

 One day, the girl who gave them their dinner – their carer – appeared in the alleyway with a stranger. He was wearing a black jacket, trousers and hat and looked very smart. Attached to his shoulder he had a machine that muttered and squawked all the time.

As they made their way through the big yard, the strange man stopped outside the cages to inspect the dogs.

Their carer called: 'Prince come here.'

Prince trotted over.

The stranger talked to Prince privately for a few minutes and then the gate was unlocked. He took out a collar and lead, which he put on the Alsatian. The gate was locked again and they walked away, with Prince following. He looked very proud and happy, calling his farewells, as he passed along the rows of cages.

What had happened?

No one knew.

The dogs in the yard talked and talked, but they didn't have an answer. Then, all of a sudden, they realised their leader had gone. They were on their own. But

Ella Morrissey, 10

Prince had trained them well. And, without any arguing or fighting, they chose Daisy to be their new leader, as she had been there longer than any of them.

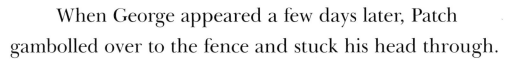

When George appeared a few days later, Patch gambolled over to the fence and stuck his head through.

'Oh George, I've so much to tell you. Prince has gone. Where did he go? And what's a police? Was the man who took him a police?'

George laughed. 'One question at a time. Can't answer you all at once.'

He looked at Patch, studying him carefully

The puppy had grown since coming to the home. His neck had healed, and his fur was re-growing and would soon hide the scar. He was no longer emaciated, either, although he was still a bit thin.

'Good – anyone can see you're better,' George said cheerfully. 'Was the man wearing a uniform and a hat? You can always recognise a policeman by his uniform. Have to treat them with respect though.'

'But George, what *is* a policeman?' demanded Patch, jumping up and down with pleasure at seeing his friend.

'A policeman,' said George, thinking hard. 'A policeman is someone who protects humans from other humans.'

'What do you mean? Why do humans need protecting from humans?' Patch asked.

'Well, you see, there are good humans and bad humans, exactly like dogs. Understand?'

Patch did. He remembered the dogs that had attacked him, and nodded.

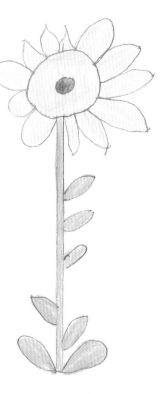

'Well, instead of fighting things out like we dogs do, humans have special men to look after them; policemen.'

'And Prince?'

'He will go to a school for police dogs, and learn how to sniff out the bad humans. Then Prince will fight the bad humans.'

Christina Hopkins, 11

'Alsatians are smart. They learn very quickly. Not like you and me, we'll never learn.' George laughed.

'But George!' Patch sounded surprised. 'You're *very* clever.'

'Not like Prince,' George replied, 'though I know a thing or two, but I'm too old now to go to school.'

But George *was* clever. Clever and sensible, and Patch learned a lot from him. He noticed how the other dogs respected him. And when George was about they were better behaved and watched their language.

Almost every day visitors arrived at the Home. Of course the dogs understood why they came. They studied the visitors closely as they walked round and round the rows of cages, gazing at the dogs, hoping to find that one special dog to take home with them.

Some dogs were much gayer, while others tried begging. But there were some dogs that pretended they didn't care and sat in the corner of their cage, with their heads turned away.

This made Patch feel very sad because he knew, deep down inside these dogs wanted a home, with fresh air and grass to roll on, the same as every other dog.

Sometimes it was lucky day and a dog was chosen. Off he would go, shouting his goodbyes, very happy and excited at the thought of the new life that was waiting for him. When that happened the dogs that were left behind were sad and quiet.

And when new dogs arrived at the home, they were often as thin and unhappy as Patch had been.

Chloë Guppy, 13

Patch watched the visitors, hoping they would choose him. But no one ever looked at him, walking straight past as if they didn't see him. It was the smaller dogs, with short fur, that people stopped to look at. And it was those dogs that were chosen first. Patch didn't know why and waited anxiously, for George's next visit, to ask him.

'George, can I ask you something?' he shouted, as soon as he spotted his friend.

'Course, old chap. What is it?' roared George. He ambled over to the yard and plonked himself down, sprawling right across the pathway, so people had to climb over him to get past.

'Why don't people ever look at me?' Patch asked sadly.

'Well, old chap, it's difficult to understand sometimes what humans want. You *are* a bit of a mongrel, you know. Humans usually go for a smallish dog with some breeding. But you've got character. One day someone will come looking for a dog with character, and off you will go.'

'But George,' begged Patch. 'What is character?'

'Well,' George scratched his ear thoughtfully. 'It's understanding things as well as humans. You see humans are often very lonely.'

'But there are hundreds of them, George!' said Patch astonished. 'I saw lots of houses on my way to the Home.'

Samuel, Cotterill, 12

George scratched his other ear. 'Yes, but humans are not like dogs. They don't talk to other humans unless they know them,' he said. 'And many humans live on their own. That's why they have a dog – to keep them company. And they need us to understand them.'

'Oh,' said Patch, not really understanding. 'Anything else,' he asked.

'And it's being cheerful,' laughed George.

Patch was still no wiser, but he wanted to be exactly like George, so he hid his unhappiness and always tried to look cheerful.

He also tried talking to the other dogs, to see what they thought about things. But he didn't pick up anything new – except a few fleas.

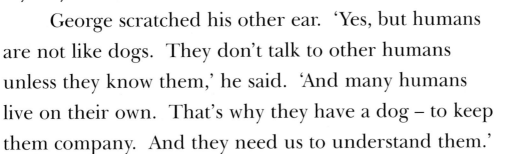

Found

 The months passed, autumn and winter came and went and Patch got used to seeing his friends find new owners and leave the home.

Now Patch was in charge of the yard. He tried to look after the new arrivals, as George and Prince had looked after him. And when the new dogs asked him: 'why are you here?' Patch wished he could say: *I'm going to be a police dog*. But all he could say was: 'I'm looking for a new home too!'

One day, when Patch had been at the home for about nine months, and spring was just around the corner, George's owner appeared with two ladies. She seemed to know them quite well and they were talking and laughing together, as they strolled along, not even looking at the dogs.

They reached the yard where Patch lived. He and George were having their usual morning chat, through the wire mesh, and lying down in order to think better.

'George,' said his owner. 'Say *Good morning*.'

George got up and held out a polite paw to the ladies, who shook it.

Patch was impressed.

'Wow, George,' he whispered.

'Wherever did you learn that? It's terrific.'

The ladies moved on down the path.

58

Kane Ingram, 12

'Oh, I forgot,' said George's owner and turned back. She took out the key for the yard and, opening it, called out to Patch. 'Here boy.'

He got up and trotted over.

'This is George's friend,' she said, 'the one I told you about. He came to us last summer in a terrible state. But, as you can see, he is quite well again. He's in charge of this yard, since he's been here the longest, and he's such a good-tempered, kindly dog.'

Patch wished desperately he could shake hands like George, but he couldn't.

One of the ladies, she was quite little, bent down and patted him.

He wanted to shout: '*Please little lady, take me with you.*' Just in time he remembered George's warning, and grinned instead.

'Look at that!' said the little lady, sounding astonished. 'He's laughing. Well, that settles it. We're taking you home.'

And before Patch could believe his whiskers, a lead was put on him and he was out of the yard. He pulled at it impatiently, wanting to get out into the sunshine.

'George,' he shouted. 'I'm going home, really going home. Goodbye everyone, good luck.'

The lady went into the office to sign some papers, with Patch, jumping up and down on his lead, his tail

whizzing round and round in circles.

George was laughing too, his great face beaming with pleasure.

'Now remember everything I've said. Be cheerful,' said the most cheerful of dogs, his bright eyes peering out through their forest of hair.

The two ladies went over to a car, Patch trotting proudly with them.

'Get in, boy,' said the little lady.

Patch didn't need telling twice. He quickly jumped onto the back seat and sat down, still unable to believe what was happening. The two ladies got into the front, the tall one driving.

'Goodbye George,' Patch shouted, and stuck his head through the window. 'Thanks. Thanks for everything. I'll miss you.'

'Goodbye, old chap,' roared George. 'Remember, keep cheerful.'

The car turned into the road and then George was gone

Annie Emery, 11

Patch watched the houses in Bristol whiz past. Soon there was just grass and trees. Big black and white animals gazed at him over hedges, and he saw white woolly animals, munching at the grass in the fields.

Sometimes he saw another dog and shouted: 'Good morning' through the car window, but they took no notice.

After a while he got bored with shouting at strange dogs, and began to listen to the ladies talking. The little one had such a kind face and a soft voice. The lady, who was driving, called her Aunty.

'Well, what are you going to call him, Aunty?' she asked.

'I don't know, Kate, he doesn't really look like anything in particular.'

'My name's Patch,' he shouted. 'But I'd like to be called George.'

'I know, old boy, but you see I don't understand.' Aunty, turned round to look at Patch on the backseat. She patted him gently and scratched his ear. 'He really is a bit scruffy though, isn't he? Never mind, old boy, when I get you home, I'll give you a bath and a brush.'

Kate laughed. 'Why not call him Scruffy?'

Aunty looked at the young dog on the back seat. 'Well, what do *you* think about that, Scruffy?'

Patch was shocked. SCRUFFY!

He was just going to protest when the little lady smiled at him.

'Well, it's okay by me, but don't tell George,' he smiled back.

'That's settled then,' Aunty patted his head. 'Goodboy, Scruffy, go to sleep now. We'll soon be home.'

Scruffy tucked his nose beneath his paw. It had been an exciting day. He had a new owner, a new name and soon he'd have a new home. And since he might as well begin his new life by obeying her, he went to sleep.

There was silence. Overhead the sun shone and the larks sang high up in the blue sky, unseen by all but the cats.

Joy leaned her face against Scruffy, her arm round his neck. Nick sat quietly thinking, his chin resting on his knees. Ginger and Cinnamon, who had heard the story many times before, lay on their side

Christie Thorn, 9

with their eyes closed and, unless you knew better, you would have thought they really were fast asleep.

Katherine Thomas, 8

'Best dinner, I ever ate,' added Scruffy licking his lips. 'That bowl of biscuits and gravy I had at George's. Best dinner I ever ate. I can still taste it.'

Suddenly Ginger leapt to his feet. 'I forgot,' he shouted. 'It's liver today. Come on, you lot. Last one in the kitchen's a cowardy custard.'

And, in a twinkling of an eye, there was nothing to be seen of the three animals, except their tails, as they chased across the lawn to get their tea.

'Do you think it's our teatime, too?' asked Joy.

'Must be,' said Nick. He stood up. 'Let's go and see. Come on, I'll race you.'

Next second the lawn was deserted.

Rose Cairns, 7

SMALL ILLUSTRATIONS
Bees, flowers and butterflies by Aletia Spencer-Jones, 8
Scruffy by Georgia Townend, 11

COVER ILLUSTRATIONS
Front cover: Holly Goldsmith, 13
Bavk cover: Roxanne Allen, 13

PARTICIPATING SCHOOLS

Bristol
Beacon Rise Primary
Torwood House Junior
Redland High Junior
Withywood Community School
The Tynings School, Staple Hill
May Park Primary, Eastville
Wellsway, Keynsham
Pucklechurch Primary
Flax Bourton Primary
Broadlands School, Keynsham
Blagdon Primary
St Mathias & Dr Bells Primary, Fishponds

Bath & N E Somerset
Newbridge Primary, Bath
Norton Hill School, Radstock
Writhlington School, Radstock
Chew Valley School, Chew Magna
St Benedicts Catholic Primary, Midsomer Norton

N. Somerset
Kingshill County Primary, Nailsea
Golden Valley Primary, Nailsea
St. Martin's Junior School, Weston S M
Mary Elton School, Clevedon

South Gloucestershire
Katharine Lady Berkeley, Wootten under Edge
Hillesley Primary, Wootten under Edge

Somerset
Castle Cary Primary
Wincanton Primary
Wells Blue School
Wells Cathedral School
Rode 1st Methodist, Frome
Ashlands C of E Primary, Crewkerne
Queens College, Taunton
Millfield Preparatory School

Somerset
Ashlands C of E First School, Crewkerne
King Alfred School, Highbridge
Greenfylds C of E Primary, Ilminster
Swanmead Community, Ilminster
Bucklers Mead Community School, Yeovil
Wellington Senior School
St Joseph's RC Primary, Bridgwater